NIM'S ISLAND

NIM'S FRIENDS

By Danielle Denega

Based on the screenplay by Joseph Kwong & Paula Mazur
and Mark Levin & Jennifer Flackett
Based on the characters created by Wendy Orr

Scholastic Inc.

New York   Toronto   London   Auckland   Sydney
Mexico City   New Delhi   Hong Kong   Buenos Aires

ISBN-13: 978-0-545-06575-7
ISBN-10: 0-545-06575-5

Published by Scholastic Inc.

WALDEN MEDIA

www.walden.com/nimsisland

12 11 10 9 8 7 6 5 4 3 2 1   8 9 10 11 12/0

Printed in the U.S.A.
First printing, April 2008

Far away in the South Pacific Ocean, there is a beautiful island that no one knows about.

Well, almost no one . . .

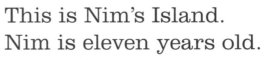

This is Nim's Island.
Nim is eleven years old.

Her dad, Jack, is a scientist.
Nim and Jack are the only people
who live on Nim's Island.

Nim and Jack built themselves a big, comfortable home out of materials from the island.

And once in a while a ship comes to bring them things they can't make for themselves, like books and packets of seeds.

It may seem like Nim would be
lonely on her island.
    But she has a way of finding
friends in unusual places. . . .

Like in the pages of her books!
Nim loves to read.

She says, "Just about everything
I know about the world comes from
inside my books."

In fact, the characters from Nim's
books are some of her closest friends.
One of Nim's best imaginary friends
is a boy named Huck Finn.

Huck and Nim have lots of fun together. They love to race each other through the jungle.

Another of Nim's imaginary friends is Alice. She comes from the book *Alice in Wonderland*.

Alice reminds Nim to be careful.
When a volcano erupts on Nim's
Island, Alice warns Nim, "Maybe it
is too dangerous here."

Even though Huck and Alice are imaginary, they are very important to Nim. And they help her defend her island from the invading tourists!

Nim's very favorite books to read are about the famous adventurer Alex Rover. He's brave, and his stories are always action-packed!

But not all of Nim's friends are from books.

"I've got plenty of real friends," Nim explains with a smile.

Nim's other friends are a little out of the ordinary though. They can swim and climb and fly . . .

They're animals!

One of her best animal friends is a sea lion named Selkie.

Instead of a teddy bear, Nim cuddles up with Selkie at night.

Nim and Selkie love to go swimming together, too!

Chica is another of Nim's friends. She is a giant sea turtle who lives in the water around Nim's Island.

When Chica's eggs begin to hatch, Nim's there to watch over them. She makes sure that Chica's baby turtles are safe.

Fred is a marine iguana that likes to bother Chica.

Fred is always nearby, often right on Nim's shoulder!

Even though Fred looks a little like a dragon, he wouldn't hurt a fly . . . unless, of course, he's eating it for breakfast!

Galileo is a pelican who soars in the skies above Nim's Island.

He lets Nim know when unusual things are going on.

Galileo is a friend to Nim's dad, too. He brings Jack tools so Jack can repair his boat.

But of all Nim's friends,
one stands out.

"I only have one best friend:
my dad," says Nim proudly.

Jack teaches Nim about lots of things. He especially loves to teach Nim about all the amazing animals and plants on their island.

He also teaches Nim about courage. He tells her, "Courage is something we have to learn and relearn our whole lives." This lesson helps Nim be strong.

Nim is very lucky to have so
many different kinds of friends.